BEEGU
Alexis Deacon

HUTCHINSON
London   Sydney   Auckland   Johannesburg

for the other
BEEGU

BEEGU
A HUTCHINSON BOOK 0 09 176829 2

Published in Great Britain by Hutchinson,
an imprint of Random House Children's Books

First published 2003

1 3 5 7 9 10 8 6 4 2

RANDOM HOUSE CHILDREN'S BOOKS
61–63 Uxbridge Road, London W5 5SA
A division of The Random House Group Ltd

RANDOM HOUSE AUSTRALIA (PTY) LTD
20 Alfred Street, Milsons Point, Sydney,
New South Wales 2061, Australia

RANDOM HOUSE NEW ZEALAND LTD
18 Poland Road, Glenfield, Auckland 10, New Zealand

RANDOM HOUSE (PTY) LTD
Endulini, 5A Jubilee Road, Parktown 2193, South Africa

THE RANDOM HOUSE GROUP Limited Reg. No. 954009
www.kidsatrandomhouse.co.uk

A CIP catalogue record for this book is available from the British Library.

Printed and bound in Singapore

Beegu was not supposed to be here.

She was lost.

No one seemed to understand her.

Some wouldn't even stay still to listen.

From far away

she thought she heard

her mother

calling . . .

RING BRING BRING BRING BRING

. . . but it wasn't her.

Beegu didn't like being alone.

She needed to find some friends.

And she did at last.

But Beegu wasn't
wanted there,
it seemed.

Then she thought she'd found
the perfect place . . .

. . . and it was!

But not everyone thought so . . .

'Wait!'

Her friends
wanted to say goodbye.

Goodbye!

Once again, from far away she thought
she heard her mother calling.
But she knew it couldn't be . . .

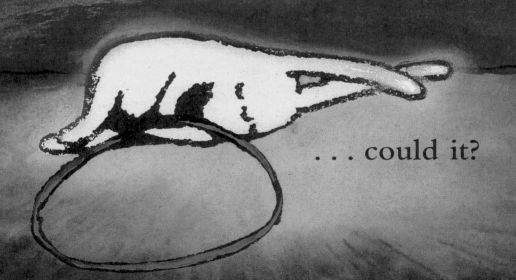

. . . could it?

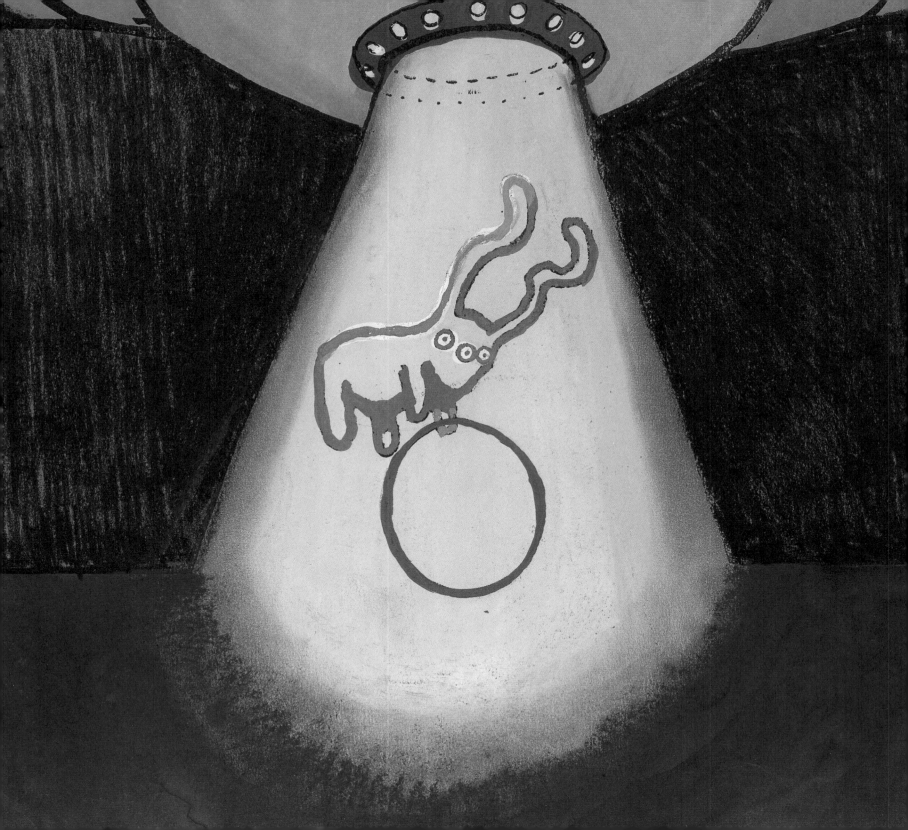

It was!

Beegu told her parents all about life
on Earth. How Earth creatures were
mostly big and unfriendly, but there
were some small ones who
seemed hopeful.

Beegu would always remember
those small ones.

She hoped they would remember her too.

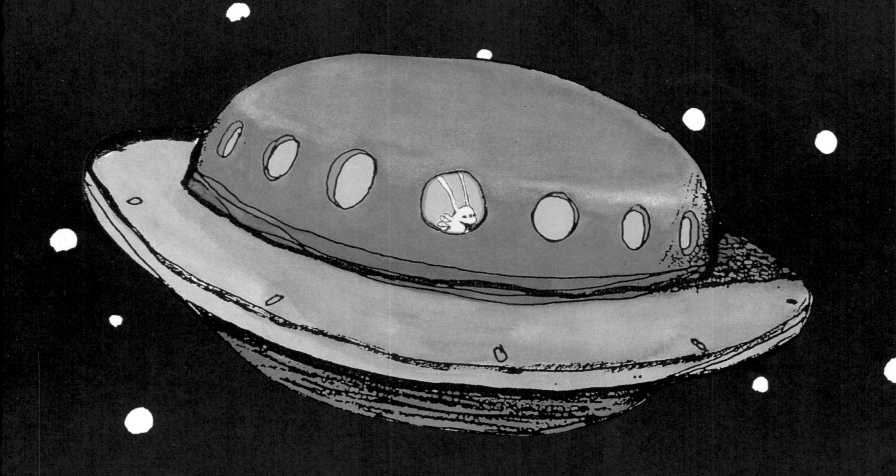

Alison • Alix • Alizee • Alizée • Allan • Alva • Alycia • Alyssia • Amaël • Amandine • Amel • Amélia • Amélie • Amil • Amy • Anaïs • Anastasia • André • Andréa • Andrew • Angéline • Angelique • Anna • Anne • Anne-Charlotte • Ann... Antonin • Antony • Antti • Aoife • Ari • Ariane • Armel • Arnaud • Arno • Arthur • Astrid • Aude • Audrey • A... ...Aurélie-Anne • Aurélien • Auréline • Aurora • Axel • Ayah • Ayumi • Baha • Bakhari • Baptiste • Barbara • Barek • Barnaby • Bart • Basile • Bastien • Béatrice • Beatrix • Bénédicte • Benjamin • Bergère • Bertille • Beryl • Billiejean • Billy • Blandine • Bouchra • Brice • Brigitte • Bruin • Callan • Calypso • Camilia • Camilla • Camille • Cansu • Carl • Carla • Carlo • Carmella • Carol-Ann • Caroline • Cassandra • Catherine • Cathy • Cécile • Cécilia • Cédric • Célina • Céline • Chandra • Chantal • Charles • Charlie • Charline • Charlotte • Charly • Chloé • Chloë • Christina • Christine • Christophe • Christopher • Ciaran • Cindy • Claire • Clara • Clémence • Clemens • Clément • Cloe • Cloé • Come • Constance • Coralie • Corentin • Corey-Joe • Cosette • Cynthia • Cyril • Cyrille • Damien • Daniel • Daniel-Gabriel • Danielle • Daphné • David • Diane • Diego • Dillon • Dimitri • Dimitry • Dominique • Dorian • Dylan • Edouard • Édouard • Edward • Edwina • Eleanor • Elena • Eléonore • Elias • Eline • Eliot • Élisa • Elisabeth • ...betta • Élise • ... • Ella • Ëlle • Ellery • Elly • Élodie • Éloi • Eloise • Éloïse • Eloïse • Elsa • Émile • Émilie • Émily • En... • Emmeline • Enzo • Eric • Éric • Erick • Estelle • Eugénie • Éva • Evan • Évelyne • Fabienne • Famory • ... • Ferdinand • Flavie • Flavien • Florence • Florent • Florian • Florine • Folra • Fournier • France • ... • François-Guillaume • Frédéric • Frédérique • Fredrik • Gabriel • Gabriella • Gabrielle • Gaë... • ...neviève • Geoffrey • Georges • Georgia • Gérard • Gilles • Giovani • Godefroy • Grégory • Guillau... • ...za • Harmonie • Harold • Harriet • Helena • Hélène • Henri • Henry • Hervé • Honor • Hugo • Hu... • ...a • Isabelle • Isaline • Ivan • Jack • Jade • Jalal • James • Jamie • Jan-Carl • Jasmin • Jason • Ja... • ...e • Jean-Claude • Jean-Didier • Jean-Édouard • Jean-François • Jean-Louis • Jean-Marc • Jean... • ...nifer • Jens • Jérémie • Jérôme • Jérôme-Édouard • Jessica • Joanna • Joël • Joëlle • Johanna • J... • ...oséphine • Joshua • Julia • Julian • Julie • Julien • Juliet • Juliette • Justine • Kalia • Karen • ...in • ...y • Kenza • Kévin • Kim • Kirstie • Laëtitia • Lara • Laura • Laure • Lauréline • Lauréna • Lauren • ...• Léo • Léonard • Léopold • Lesly • Lila • Lilian • Lindsay • Lionel • Lis • Lisa • Lise-Astrid • L... • ...Louis • Louis-Arnaud • Louis-Lech • Lowellyn • Luc • Lucas • Lucie • Lucien • Lucile • Lu... • ...ydia • Lydie • Macon • Madeleine • Madeline • Madyson • Maëliss • Maëlle • Maëva • Mafal... • ...el • Marc • Marc-Antoine • Marceau • Marco • Marcus • Margaux • Margot • Marguerite • Mar... • ...Marie • Marie-Alice • Marie-Charlotte • Marie-Claire • Marie-Claude • Marie-Dominique • M... • ...Marie-Liesse • Marie-Noëlle • Marin • Marina • Marine • Marion • Marjorie • Mark-Antonin • ...• ...Massimiliano • Mateusz • Mathew • Mathias • Mathieu • Mathilde • Mathis • Matthieu • Maud... • ...imilien • Maxine • Médéric • Medhi • Megan • Mégane • Mélanie • Mélisande • Melissa • Me... • ...el • Michèle • Mickaël • Mirella • Miriam • Mohamed • Molly • Monia • Monique • Moi... • ...nam • Nadège • Nadia • Nancy • Narayan • Nashilu • Natacha • Natascha • Natasha • Nathalie • Nath... • ...st • N... • Nestor • Nicholas • Nicolas • Nicole • Nina • Niroshan • Noémie • Nolan • Nolwenn • Nora • ...Oliver • O... • Olivier • Ophélie • Oriane • Owen • Palmyre • Pascal • Patrice • Patrick • Paul • Pauline • Pe... • ...ippa • Philippe • Philippine • Pierre • Pierre-Alexandre • Pierre-Antoine • Pierre-Louis • Piers • Prentis • Préscili... • ...achel • Rachelle • ...lph • Raphaël • Rasha • Régis • Rémi • Remy • Renaud • Rodolphe • Romain • Ronan • Rosie • Ro... • ...adio • Safae • Salima • Sam • Samuel • Sandra • Sandy • Santa • Sara • Sarah • Saskia • Saul • Scharhazade • Sean • Sebastian • Sebastien • Sébastien • Séréna • Séverine • Sezgin • Shane • Sherlley • Sherzad • Sherzad • Shivani • Sibylle • Sigrid • Simon • Sofiane • Solal • Sophia • Sophian • Sophie • Soukaina • Soulaima • Steeve • Steeven • Steffie • Stéphane • Stéphanie • Suéva • Suzon • Sven • Swann • Sybille • Sylvie • Tamer • Tanguy • Teddy • Terence • Teven • Theo • Théo • Thibault • Thierry • Thomas • Thyphaine • Tidiou • Tifany • Tiffany • Timothy • Timour • Tiphaine • Tiphany • Tiril • Toby • Tom • Tommy • Tony • Tyler • Ulysse • Valentin • Valentine • Valérie • Vanessa • Vanille • Varick • Vera • Veronica • Véronique • Vianney • Victor • Victoria • Vincent • Virginia • Virginie • Vladimir • Wael • Wahidah • Wallis • Wendy • Wesley • William • Xavier • Yacine • Yael • Yanaëlle • Yannick • Yasmina • Yoana • Yoann • Yohan • Yohann • Yolande • Zineb • Zineb • Zoé • Adam • Adèle • Adrian • Adrien • Afsaneh Sophia • Agathe • Agnès • Aïcha • Alain • Alan • Alastair • Alban • Aleksandra • Alessandra • Alex • Alexander • Alexandra • Alexandre • Alexia • Alexis • Alice • Alicia • Aliénor • Alina • Aline • Alison • Alix • Alizee • Alizée • Allan • Alva • Alycia • Alyssia • Amaël • Amandine • Amel • Amélia • Amélie • Amil • Amy • Anaïs • Anastasia • André • Andréa • Andrew • Angéline • Angelique • Anna

A Sailing Boat in the Sky
A JONATHAN CAPE BOOK: 0 224 06454 1

Published in Great Britain by Jonathan Cape,
an imprint of Random House Children's Books

This edition published 2002

1 3 5 7 9 10 8 6 4 2

Copyright © Editions Rue du monde 2000
Translation © Quentin Blake 2002

RANDOM HOUSE CHILDREN'S BOOKS
61-63 Uxbridge Road, London W5 5SA
A division of The Random House Group Ltd.

RANDOM HOUSE AUSTRALIA (PTY) LTD
20 Alfred Street, Milsons Point, Sydney,
New South Wales 2061, Australia

RANDOM HOUSE NEW ZEALAND LTD
18 Poland Road, Glenfield, Auckland 10, New Zealand

RANDOM HOUSE (PTY) LTD
Endulini, 5A Jubilee Road, Parktown 2193, South Africa

THE RANDOM HOUSE GROUP Limited Reg. No. 954009
www.randomhouse.co.uk

A CIP catalogue record for this book is available from the British Library.

Printed and bound in Singapore by Tien Wah Press (PTE) Ltd

Quentin Blake

A Sailing Boat in the Sky

Jonathan Cape
London

Isobel and Nicholas were walking along the beach,
chatting about nothing in particular.
It was just an ordinary day.

That is, until they reached the top of the dune.

'Look, Nick,' said Isobel.
'It's a boat, but it's all broken up.
What do you think – shall we try
to put it back together again?'

The parts of the boat were all there,
and Isobel and Nicholas set about
trying to piece them together.

'These wheels seem to fit on the side,' said Nicholas.
'It's a very funny sort of boat.'

They climbed in. The wind blew and the old sails filled
and slowly, the boat began to roll along the beach.
'Strange looking bird on the port bow!' shouted Isobel.

'Nothing strange about me,' said the bird.
'I'm just a stork and my name is Simona.
But I've been shot in the wing and so I can't fly.'

Just then the wind blew harder,
and the boat picked up speed.

'Quick!' said Isobel. 'Get in!'

They just managed to catch hold of Simona
as the boat rolled along faster and faster
and took off into the sky.

They found themselves
in the middle of a flock
of birds who all looked
very like Simona.

The biggest of the storks flew alongside them. 'My name's Gus,' he said.
'Now that you've rescued our Simona, what about helping others?
I can see plenty of people who need saving from up here.'
'What about it?' Nicholas said to Isobel.
'Why not?' she replied. 'Let's go!'

They sailed on, over beach after beach,
and then suddenly, below them, they saw a girl
running away from a group of children who were
throwing stones at her and calling her names.
'Quick!' said Simona. 'Before they hit her on the wing!'

The stones bounced off the boat as Isobel and Nicholas
helped the girl on board. Her name was Eloise.
'Why do they want to hurt me?' she sobbed.
'I haven't done anything wrong.'

On and on they flew, until they came across
a troubling sight. A group of men
were hacking away at rocks with pickaxes,
and amongst them were several small boys
trying to do the same.

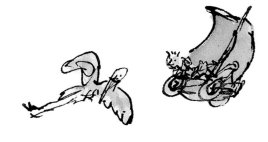

One of them was so weak
that he could not even stand.

As they flew over, Isobel and Nicholas
just managed to grab the boy by the hands
before the boat moved off.

Their new friend was called Rachid.
He had a ragged scarf around his neck,
which Eloise used to wipe away the sweat
from his forehead as they sailed on through the sky.

But then, 'Oh, no,' said Isobel. 'What's this horrible
dark cloud in front of us?'

They were over a town where everything smoked:
the houses, the factories, the cars and even the people.
Soon everyone in the boat was coughing and holding their noses.
'It may be bad for us,' said Isobel, 'but look at that poor boy
down there. He can't breathe at all.'

'Hold on,' said Gus.
   'Let me try to help him.'

The boy was called Eric, and he was so happy
to be able to breathe again. They all felt much better
as they sailed peacefully through the bright clear sky.

'But what's that noise?' said Nicholas.
'Is it some kind of storm?'

It wasn't a storm.

It was warplanes, rockets and deafening
explosions. They were in a war zone.
'We've got to get out of here!' cried Isobel.
'But wait!' she said. 'We must try to save
that woman and her baby.'

The woman told them that her name was Magda
and that her baby was called Lira.
All hands were needed to help them safely aboard.

But they were not safe yet . . .

There were holes in the boat, the sails were torn
and there were so many people on board
that it was sinking lower and lower in the sky.
'We must find somewhere to land soon,' said Nicholas.
'But where?'

At last they came to another beach.
'How about there?' suggested Gus.
'We can't land there,' said Nicholas. 'Look at that
awful woman with the green face. Do you
think she's a witch?'

'Don't be silly,' said Eloise. 'There's nothing
to be afraid of. She's my granny and she sells fish
on the beach. Everybody thinks she's lovely.'

They all busied themselves taking the boat to pieces.
Upside down the hull made a shelter
where Magda and Lira could rest.
Isobel and Eric hung the sails up
to make a hammock.

Nicholas turned one set of wheels into a sort of washing line,
and Simona and Gus used the other for a nest.

Rachid collected wood for the fire,
and Eloise helped her granny
with the cooking.

The fish soup that night was very good. Eloise's granny had
added a few special ingredients, including a flying fish
to help Simona's wing get better quickly.
'It would be lovely if you could all stay here with me a bit longer,' she said.
'Yes, but how can we?' said Nicholas. 'We've got our parents.'
'And friends,' added Rachid, 'a long way from here.'
'And a lot of journeys still to make,' said Gus.
It was at that moment that Rachid noticed a ruined cabin
at the end of the beach.

'Look, with all those planks we could build
another boat – a much, much, bigger one!'
'And I know what,' said Eloise's granny.
'I can stitch together all my old dresses,
my curtains and my handkerchiefs,
and you'll have the most
beautiful sails in the world!'

And so one bright morning, when Simona
was able to fly again, there was an amazing
new sailing boat in the sky.

And what happened after that, you will just have to imagine . . .

This book has Quentin Blake's name on the front of it, but he did not do it all by himself. He had helpers: 1,800 children from many parts of the world, including London, Singapore, Dublin, Luxembourg, Oslo (you can read their names on the endpapers).

The adventure began in the southwest of France, where Quentin Blake spends part of every year and where a group of local teachers invited him to work with their young pupils on a book about the problems of our world – problems such as prejudice, pollution, child slavery and war. He started them off with three rough drawings and then, throughout an entire school year, the teachers set in order an avalanche of ideas and suggestions, words and pictures. There were discussions in class, exchanges on the Internet, and in France there were gatherings of hundreds of children where Quentin Blake explained and encouraged and they read their poems, sang and performed. Listening to what they had to say, following their words and pictures in front of him, Quentin Blake produced *A Sailing Boat in the Sky* – a book that, like the boat it describes, can now set off to meet other children and invite their thoughts and hopes about the future and the way we should live together.

Adam • Adèle • Adrian • Adrien • Afsaneh Sophia • Agathe • Agnès • Aïcha • Alain • Alan • Alastair • Alban • Aleksandra • Alessandra • Alex • Alexander • Alexandra • Alexandre • Alexia • Alexis • Alice • Alicia • Aliénor • Alina • Aline • Alison • Alix • Alizee • Alizée • Allan • Alva • Alycia • Alyssia • Amaël • Amandine • Amel • Amélia • Amélie • Amil • Amy • Anaïs • Anastasia • André • Andréa • Andrew • Angéline • Angelique • Anna • Anne • Anne-Charlotte • Annie • Anthony • Antoine • Antonin • Antony • Antti • Aoife • Ari • Ariane • Armel • Arnaud • Arno • Arthur • Astrid • Aude • Audrey • August • Augustin • Aurélie • Aurélie-Anne • Aurélien • Auréline • Aurora • Axel • Ayah • Ayumi • Baha • Bakhari • Baptiste • Barbara • Barek • Barnaby • Bart • Basile • Bastien • Béatrice • Beatrix • Bénédicte • Benjamin • Bergère • Bertille • Beryl • Billiejean • Billy • Blandine • Bouchra • Brice • Brigitte • Bruin • Callan • Calypso • Camilia • Camilla • Camille • Cansu • Carl • Carla • Carlo • Carmella • Carol-Ann • Caroline • Cassandra • Catherine • Cathy • Cécile • Cécilia • Cédric • Célina • Céline • Chandra • Chantal • Charles • Charlie • Charline • Charlotte • Charly • Chloé • Chloë • Christina • Christine • Christophe • Christopher • Ciaran • Cindy • Claire • Clara • Clémence • Clemens • Clément • Cloe • Cloé • Come • Constance • Coralie • Corentin • Corey-Joe • Cosette • Cynthia • Cyril • Cyrille • Damien • Daniel • Daniel-Gabriel • Danielle • Daphné • David • Diane • Diego • Dillon • Dimitri • Dimitry • Dominique • Dorian • Dylan • Edouard • Édouard • Edward • Edwina • Eleanor • Elena • Eléonore • Elias • Eline • Eliot • Élisa • Elisabeth • Elisabetta • Élise • Elisha • Ella • Ëlle • Ellery • Elly • Élodie • Éloi • Eloise • Éloïse • Eloïse • Elsa • Émile • Émilie • Émily • Emma • Emmanuel • Emmanuelle • Emmeline • Enzo • Eric • Éric • Erick • Estelle • Eugénie • Éva • Evan • Évelyne • Fabienne • Famory • Fanny • Farid • Faustine • Félix • Ferdinand • Flavie • Flavien • Florence • Florent • Florian • Florine • Folra • Fournier • France • Francesca • Francis • François • Françoise • François-Guillaume • Frédéric • Frédérique • Fredrik • Gabriel • Gabriella • Gabrielle • Gaëtan • Garance • Gauthier • Gemma • Geneviève • Geoffrey • Georges • Georgia • Gérard • Gilles • Giovani • Godefroy • Grégory • Guillaume • Gwendal • Hadrien • Hamish • Hamza • Harmonie • Harold • Harriet • Helena • Hélène • Henri • Henry • Hervé • Honor • Hugo • Hussein • Ian • Ida • India • Ines • Ingrid • Irina • Isabelle • Isaline • Ivan • Jack • Jade • Jalal • James • Jamie • Jan-Carl • Jasmin • Jason • Jasper • Jean • Jean-Baptiste • Jean-Christophe • Jean-Claude • Jean-Didier • Jean-Édouard • Jean-François • Jean-Louis • Jean-Marc • Jean-Marie • Jean-Noël • Jedjigha • Jenna • Jennifer • Jens • Jérémie • Jérôme • Jérôme-Édouard • Jessica • Joanna • Joël • Joëlle • Johanna • John • Jonas • Jonathan • Jordi • Joseph • Joséphine • Joshua • Julia • Julian • Julie • Julien • Juliet • Juliette • Justine • Kalia • Karen • Karima • Katherin • KeelanAnge • Kelly • Keny • Kenza • Kévin • Kim • Kirstie • Laëtitia • Lara • Laura • Laure • Lauréline • Lauréna • Laurence • Laurent • Laurie • Léa • Leila • Léna • Léo • Léonard • Léopold • Lesly • Lila • Lilian • Lindsay • Lionel • Lis • Lisa • Lise-Astrid • Logan • Loïc • Lola • Lolita • Lorcan • Lorie • Louis • Louis-Arnaud • Louis-Lech • Lowellyn • Luc • Lucas • Lucie • Lucien • Lucile • Lucile–Isabelle • Lucy • Ludovic • Luke • Lydia • Lydie • Macon • Madeleine • Madeline • Madyson • Maëliss • Maëlle • Maëva • Mafalda • Magdalena • Magnus • Manon • Manuel • Marc • Marc-Antoine • Marceau • Marco • Marcus • Margaux • Margot • Marguerite • Maria • Maria-Isabel • Maria-Luisa • Marianne • Marie • Marie-Alice • Marie-Charlotte • Marie-Claire • Marie-Claude • Marie-Dominique • Marie-Eugénie • Mariefer • Marie-Jeanne • Marie-Liesse • Marie-Noëlle • Marin • Marina • Marine • Marion • Marjorie • Mark-Antonin • Marlène • Marte • Martine • Maryline • Massimiliano • Mateusz • Mathew • Mathias • Mathieu • Mathilde • Mathis • Matthieu • Maud • Maureen • Max • Maxim • Maxime • Maximilien • Maxine • Médéric • Medhi • Megan • Mégane • Mélanie • Mélisande • Melissa • Mélodie • Mercedes • Michael • Michaël • Michel • Michèle • Mickaël • Mirella • Miriam • Mohamed • Molly • Monia • Monique • Morgan • Morgane • Mukâyil • Murray • Myriam • Nadège • Nadia • Nancy • Narayan • Nashilu • Natacha • Natascha • Natasha • Nathalie • Nathan • Nathanaël • Nathanaël-Margot • Nesrin • Nestor • Nicholas • Nicolas • Nicole • Nina • Niroshan • Noémie • Nolan • Nolwenn • Nora • Océane • Odile • Ola • Olav • Oliver • Olivia • Olivier • Ophélie • Oriane • Owen • Palmyre • Pascal • Patrice • Patrick • Paul • Pauline • Pélagie • Peter • Philip • Philippa • Philippe • Philippine • Pierre • Pierre-Alexandre • Pierre-Antoine • Pierre-Louis • Piers • Prentis • Préscilia • Priscilla • Quentin • Rachel • Rachelle • Ralph • Raphaël • Rasha • Régis • Rémi • Remy • Renaud • Rodolphe • Romain • Ronan • Rosie • Roxanne • Sabrina • Sadio • Safae • Salima • Sam • Samuel • Sandra • Sandy • Santa • Sara • Sarah • Saskia • Saul • Scharhazade • Sean • Sebastian • Sebastien • Sébastien • Séréna • Séverine • Sezgin • Shane • Sherlley • Sherzad • Sherzad • Shivani • Sibylle • Sigrid • Simon • Sofiane • Solal • Sophia • Sophian • Sophie • Soukaina • Soulaima • Steeve • Steeven • Steffie • Stéphane • Stéphanie • Suéva • Suzon • Sven • Swann • Sybille • Sylvie • Tamer • Tanguy • Teddy • Terence • Teven • Theo • Théo • Thibault • Thierry • Thomas • Thyphaine • Tidiou • Tifann • Tiffany • Timothy • Timour • Tiphaine • Tiphany • Tiril • Toby • Tom • Tommy • Tony • Tyler • Ulysse • Valentin • Valentine • Valérie • Vanessa • Vanille • Varick • Vera • Veronica • Véronique • Vianney • Victor • Victoria • Vincent • Virginia • Virginie • Vladimir • Wael • Wahidah • Wallis • Wendy • Wesley • William • Xavier • Yacine • Yael • Yanaëlle • Yannick • Yasmina • Yoana • Yoann • Yohan • Yohann • Yolande • Zineb • Zineb • Zoé • Adam • Adèle • Adrian • Adrien • Afsaneh Sophia • Agathe • Agnès • Aïcha • Alain • Alan • Alastair • Alban • Aleksandra • Alessandra • Alex • Alexander • Alexandra • Alexandre • Alexia • Alexis • Alice • Alicia • Aliénor • Alina • Aline